Text copyright © 2008 by Anke de Vries

Illustrations copyright © 2008 by Charlotte Dematons

Originally published in the Netherlands by Lemniscaat b.v. Rotterdam, 2008,
 under the title *Raf*

All rights reserved

Printed in Belgium

First U.S. edition, 2009

ISBN: 978-1-59078-749-6

CIP data is available.

Lemniscaat

An Imprint of Boyds Mills Press, Inc.

815 Church Street

Honesdale, Pennsylvania 18431

RAF

Anke de Vries &
Charlotte Dematons

Lemniscaat
Honesdale, Pennsylvania

Ben and Raf are always together.
Wherever Ben goes, Raf goes with him.

One day, Raf is gone.
Ben looks everywhere,
but Raf is nowhere to be found.

That night, Ben goes to bed sad—all alone.

The next morning, snow covers the ground.
Ben doesn't feel like going outside.
Without Raf, snow is no fun.

Then the mailbox clatters.

Dear Ben,

I've been found! I am
traveling through Africa.
Right now, I am in the desert.
It is really hot. The sun burns
my head. I am as brown as
chocolate.

Raf

Benjamin
Berenstraat
Holland

Dear Ben,

Now I am at a big lake, floating between a bunch of pink birds. Do you know what they are called?

P.S. Help! They are pooping on my nose.

Raf

Benjamin
Berenstraat
Holland

Hi, Ben!

The pink birds all flew
away. The elephants scared
them.

I wasn't afraid at all. I had
a nice shower. When I dried
myself in the sun, I shrank
a little.

Raf

Benjamin
Berenstraat
Holland

Hey there, Ben!

I wish you were here in
the jungle, too.
I've been swinging on
vines with the monkeys.
All that swinging has
made my neck and tail a little
longer.

Raf

Benjamin
Berenstraat
Holland

Dear Ben,

You won't believe it!
I am visiting the giraffes.
They made me stay for
dinner.

African food is good!
I couldn't get enough of it.

Raf

Benjamin

Berenstraat

Holland

Hooray, hooray, hooray!

   We are coming back. I have changed a bit. You may not recognize me.
   I can't wait to see you again. How about you?

Raf

Benjamin
Berenstraat
Holland

Days go by. No more postcards arrive.
Did Raf forget about Ben?

Tomorrow is Ben's birthday.

Ben wakes up—all alone.
Without Raf, a birthday is no fun.

RING! The doorbell rings.
Who could that be?

Benjamin
Berenstr
Holland